Disney
PRINCESS
Aladdin

Adaptation by R. J. Cregg
Translation by Laura Collado Píriz
Illustrated by the Disney Storybook Art Team

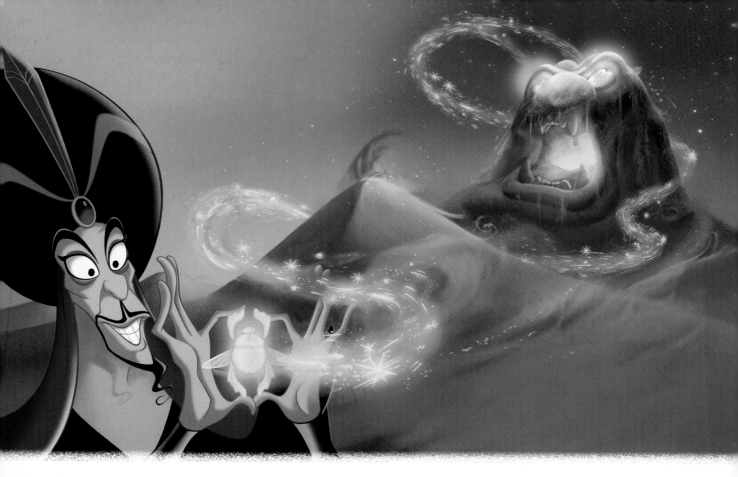

BuzzPop

An imprint of Bonnier Publishing USA
251 Park Avenue South, New York, NY 10010
BuzzPop is a trademark of Bonnier Publishing USA, and associated
colophon is a trademark of Bonnier Publishing USA.
Manufactured in China   HUH 0119
First Edition
10 9 8 7 6 5 4 3 2 1
ISBN 978-1-4998-0943-5
buzzpopbooks.com
bonnierpublishingusa.com

Érase una vez, un hechicero sediento de poder llamado Jafar que fue al **desierto** y abrió una cámara mágica llamada la Cueva de las Maravillas.
Once upon a time, a power-hungry sorcerer named Jafar went into the **desert** and opened a magical chamber, the Cave of Wonders.

Su ayudante intentó entrar, pero una voz misteriosa dijo que solo podía entrar una persona: el **diamante** en bruto.
As his helper stepped through the entrance, a mystical voice said, "Only one may enter—the **diamond** in the rough."

Entonces, la abertura se hundió en la **arena** y desapareció.
Then the opening sank into the **sand** and disappeared.

—Tengo que **encontrar** a esa persona… al diamante en bruto —dijo Jafar.
"I must **find** this one, this 'diamond in the rough,'" said Jafar.

Al **día** siguiente todo empezó como de costumbre en la cercana ciudad de Agrabah.
The next **day** started like any other in the nearby town of Agrabah.

Aladdín robó una hogaza de **pan** en el mercado.
Aladdin stole a loaf of **bread** from the marketplace.

—¡Detente, ladrón! —le gritó el **guardia** real del Sultán a Aladdín.
"Stop, thief!" the Sultan's royal **guard** shouted at Aladdin.

Aladdín tenía que **robar** para sobrevivir porque no tenía una familia para ayudarle.
Without a family to help him, Aladdin had to **steal** to eat.

En el palacio real, el buen Sultán intentaba convencer a su hija de que tenía que **casarse**.
In the royal palace, the good Sultan tried to convince his daughter it was time for her to **marry**.

—¡Pero nunca he cruzado los muros de **palacio**! —dijo la princesa Jasmín mientras abrazaba a su tigre, Rajá.
"But I've never even been outside the **palace** walls," Princess Jasmine said, while cuddling her pet tiger, Rajah.

El Sultán no **entendía** por qué Jasmín no era feliz.
The Sultan did not **understand** why Jasmine was unhappy.

A la mañana siguiente, muy temprano, Jasmín escaló el **muro** de palacio y se fue al mercado.

Early the next morning, Jasmine climbed over the palace **wall** and went to the marketplace.

Fingió ser una **plebeya** y conoció a Aladdín y a su mono, Abú.

She pretended to be a **commoner** and met Aladdin and his pet monkey, Abu.

Aladdín le dijo que se sentía **atrapado** porque tenía que vivir en la calle.

Aladdin told her he felt **trapped** because he had to live on the streets.

Jasmín también se sentía atrapada porque siempre había sido una **princesa**.

Jasmine felt trapped, too, because she had always been a **princess**.

Mientras tanto, Jafar estaba trazando un **plan** secreto para convertirse en sultán.
Meanwhile, Jafar worked on his secret **plan** to become sultan.

Necesitaba la ayuda de una **lámpara mágica** de la Cueva de las Maravillas.
He needed a **magic lamp** from the Cave of Wonders to help him.

Usó su **brujería** para descubrir quién era la persona que podía conseguir la lámpara, el "diamante en bruto".
He used **sorcery** to reveal the one who could fetch the lamp, the "diamond in the rough."

¡**Era** Aladdín!
It **was** Aladdin!

Jafar era el gran visir y envió a los guardias de palacio a **arrestar** a Aladdín.
Jafar was the royal vizier and sent the palace guards to **arrest** Aladdin.

Jasmín descubrió su verdadera **identidad** y les ordenó a los soldados que liberasen a Aladdín.
Jasmine revealed her true **identity** and ordered the soldiers to let Aladdin go.

A Aladdín le **sorprendió** mucho que Jasmín fuera la princesa.
Aladdin was **stunned** to learn that Jasmine was the princess.

Los guardias estaban obligados a seguir las **órdenes** del gran visir, así que se llevaron a Aladdín.
The men, forced to follow the royal vizier's **orders**, took Aladdin away.

Cuando Aladdín estaba en el **calabozo**, Jafar se disfrazó de viejo y se acercó a él.
Once Aladdin was in the **dungeon**, Jafar disguised himself as an old man and approached him.

Aladdín se lamentó de que un huérfano **pobre** como él nunca podría casarse con la princesa Jasmín.
Aladdin despaired that a **poor** orphan like him could never marry Princess Jasmine.

Jafar le dijo a Aladdín que podría impresionar a la princesa si fuera tan **rico** como un príncipe.
Jafar told Aladdin that he could impress the princess if he were as **rich** as a prince.

Jafar le dijo a Aladdín que le haría rico si él le hacía un **pequeño** favor.
Jafar offered to make Aladdin rich if he would do him one **small** favor.

Aladdín aceptó y Jafar le condujo fuera del calabozo por una escalera **escondida**.
Aladdin agreed and Jafar led him out of the dungeon through a **hidden** staircase.

Jafar llevó a Aladdín a la Cueva de las **Maravillas**.
Jafar brought Aladdin to the Cave of **Wonders**.

—¡Primero, traéme la lámpara! Luego podrás **tocar** el tesoro —le dijo Jafar.
"First, bring me the lamp! Then you may **touch** the treasure," Jafar called.

Aladdín descendió por los escalones y se maravilló de las **riquezas**.
Aladdin descended the steps and marveled at the **riches**.

Mientras buscaba la lámpara, una **alfombra mágica** lo siguió.
As he searched for the lamp, a **magic carpet** followed him.

La alfombra mágica llevó a Aladdín junto a la **lámpara**.
The magic carpet brought Aladdin to the **lamp**.

No parecía muy **valiosa**.
It didn't look **valuable**.

Aladdín se preguntó por qué la quería el **viejo**.
Aladdin wondered why the **old man** wanted it.

Pero Abú tocó un **enorme** rubí por su cuenta.
Off by himself, Abu picked up an **enormous** ruby.

—¡Has tocado el tesoro **prohibido**! —estalló una misteriosa voz.
"You have touched the **forbidden** treasure!" boomed a mystical voice.

La cueva se agitó y la alfombra intentó **correr** para poner a salvo a
Aladdín y a Abú.
The cave shook, and the carpet tried to **race** Aladdin and Abu to safety.

Pero la **entrada** se cerró y atrapó en la cueva a Aladdín, la lámpara, Abú y la alfombra mágica.

But the **entrance** shut, trapping Aladdin, the lamp, Abu, and the magic carpet inside the cave.

Aladdín limpió algunas manchas de la lámpara ¡y apareció un **genio**!

Aladdin rubbed some tarnish off of the lamp and a **genie** appeared!

El Genio le explicó que, como Aladdín era el amo de la lámpara, podría concederle **tres** deseos.

The Genie explained that he could grant Aladdin, the master of the lamp, **three** wishes.

Aladdín **engañó** al Genio para que les sacara de la cueva.
Aladdin **tricked** the Genie into helping them escape the cave.

Luego, Aladdín deseó ser un **príncipe** rico.
Then, Aladdin wished to be a rich **prince**.

El Genio le concedió el **deseo** y convirtió a Aladdín en el impresionante príncipe Alí.
The Genie granted the **wish**, turning Aladdin into the fabulous Prince Ali.

Aladdín **prometió** que después de que se ganara el corazón de Jasmín usaría un deseo para liberar al Genio.
Aladdin **promised** that after he won Jasmine's heart, he would use a wish to set the Genie free.

El Genio convirtió a Abú en un **elefante** y preparó un gran espectáculo para la entrada del príncipe Alí en Agrabah.
The Genie turned Abu into an **elephant** and provided great fanfare for Prince Ali's entrance into Agrabah.

Jafar y Jasmín no **reconocieron** a Aladdín y a ninguno de los dos les gustó el príncipe Alí.
Jafar and Jasmine did not **recognize** Aladdin, nor did they like Prince Ali.

Aladdín **tenía miedo** de decirle a Jasmín quién era en realidad.
Aladdin **was afraid** to tell Jasmine who he really was.

En vez de eso, le ofreció a Jasmín un **viaje** en alfombra mágica para que pudiera ver el mundo.
Instead, he offered to take Jasmine on a magic carpet **ride** so she could see the world.

Jasmín **deseó** que el viaje durase para siempre.
Jasmine **wished** their journey would never end.

Mientras se elevaban por cielo, Jasmín se **enamoró** del príncipe Alí.
As they soared through the sky, Jasmine **fell in love** with Prince Ali.

Sin la lámpara mágica, Jafar solo tenía una **manera** de convertirse en sultán.
Without the magic lamp, Jafar had only one **way** to become sultan.

Tenía que **casarse** con la princesa Jasmín.
He had to **marry** Princess Jasmine.

Primero tiró al **océano** al príncipe Alí.
First, he had Prince Ali thrown into the **ocean**.

Cuando la mano de Aladdín tocó la lámpara mágica, el Genio usó el **segundo** deseo de Aladdín para salvarle la vida.
When Aladdin's hand brushed against the magic lamp, the Genie used Aladdin's **second** wish to save his life.

Aladdín volvió al **palacio** para revelar al Sultán lo que había hecho Jafar.
Aladdin returned to the **palace** to tell the Sultan what Jafar had done.

Pero Jafar **hipnotizó** al Sultán en secreto para que creyera lo que él dijera.
But Jafar secretly **hypnotized** the Sultan into believing whatever he said.

Jafar **se preguntó** cómo había conseguido escapar el príncipe Alí.
Jafar **wondered** how Prince Ali had managed to escape.

Jafar envió a su **loro**, Iago, para espiar al príncipe Alí.
Jafar sent his pet **parrot**, Iago, to spy on Prince Ali.

Iago encontró la **lámpara** y se la llevó a Jafar.
Iago found the **lamp** and brought it to Jafar.

Jafar frotó la lámpara riéndose **como un maníaco** y apareció el Genio.
Laughing **maniacally**, Jafar rubbed the lamp and the Genie appeared.

Primero, Jafar deseó ser el **sultán**.
First, Jafar wished to be **sultan**.

Después, deseó ser el **hechicero** más poderoso del mundo.
Second, he wished to be the most powerful **sorcerer** in the world.

El Genio le concedió su deseo a su nuevo **amo** con tristeza.
Unhappily, the Genie granted the wishes of his new **master**.

Jafar usó sus poderes para **atrapar** a Jasmín en un reloj de arena y para convertir al príncipe Alí otra vez en Aladdín.
Jafar used his power to **trap** Jasmine in an hourglass and turn Prince Ali back into Aladdin.

—El Genio tiene más **poder** del que tú tendrás jamás —le dijo Aladdín sabiamente a Jafar.
"The Genie has more **power** than you'll ever have," Aladdin cleverly said to Jafar.

Jafar usó su tercer **deseo** para convertirse en un poderoso genio.
Jafar used his third **wish** to become an all-powerful genie.

Luego, como todos los genios, Jafar fue **aprisionado** en una lámpara mágica.
Then, like all genies, Jafar was **imprisoned** inside a magic lamp.

Con Jafar atrapado para siempre, Aladdín volvió a ser el **amo** de la lámpara.
With Jafar trapped forever, Aladdin was once again **master** of the lamp.

Como prometió, Aladdín usó su **último** deseo para concederle la libertad al Genio.
As promised, Aladdin used his **last** wish to set the Genie free.

El Genio estaba muy emocionado por ver el **mundo**, pero siempre sería el amigo de Aladdín y Jasmín.
The Genie was excited to see the **world**, but he would always be Jasmine and Aladdin's friend.

Aladdín **pidió disculpas** a Jasmín por fingir ser el príncipe Alí.
Aladdin **apologized** to Jasmine for pretending to be Prince Ali.

Jasmín decidió que su **aventura** no había hecho más que
empezar con su verdadero amor: Aladdín, el diamante en bruto.
Jasmine decided her **adventure** was just beginning with her true
love, Aladdin, the diamond in the rough.